KB067495

홀리데이 홈

〈K-픽션〉 시리즈는 한국문학의 젊은 상상력입니다. 최근 발표된 가장 우수하고 흥미로운 작품을 엄선하여 출간하는 〈K-픽션〉은 한국문학의 생생한 현장을 국내외 독자들과 실시간으로 공유하고자 기획되었습니다. 〈바이링궐 에디션 한국 대표 소설〉 시리즈를 통해 검증된 탁월한 번역진이 참여하여 원작의 재미와 품격을 최대한 살린 〈K-픽션〉 시리즈는 매 계절마다 새로운 작품을 선보입니다.

The K-Fiction Series represents the brightest of young imaginative voices in contemporary Korean fiction. This series spans a wide range of outstanding short stories selected by the editorial board of *ASIA* each season. These stories are then translated by professional Korean literature translators, all of whom take special care to convey the writers' original tones and nuances. We hope that these exceptional young Korean voices will delight all readers both here and abroad.

홀리데이 홈
Holiday Home

편혜영 | 김소라 옮김
Written by Pyun Hye-young
Translated by Sora Kim-Russell

ASIA
PUBLISHERS

차례

Contents

홀리데이 홈
Holiday Home

k

이진수는 군인이었다. 보자마자 알 수 있었다. 소개해준 사람이 말해주어서는 아니었다. 군복이나 관등성명 없이도 군인처럼 보였다. 장소령은 그게 별로였다. 그런데도 이진수가 함께 저녁을 먹자고 하자 고개를 끄덕였다. 이름 때문이었다.

"저도 이다음엔 소령이 됩니다."

막 대위가 되었다는 이진수가 들뜬 표정으로 말했고, 장소령은 그의 짧은 머리와 까맣게 탄 얼굴을 보며 조금 웃었다. 사시미 세트를 주문했는데 비교적 질 좋은 우니가 포함되어 있었다. 장소령은 우니를 입에 넣어 천천히 녹여 먹었다. 이진수는 그것을 지켜보았고 식사

Yi Jinsu was a soldier. She could tell at once. It wasn't that the person who set them up had told her so. He simply looked like a soldier, even without wearing a uniform or stating his rank and name. Which Jang Soryeong wasn't thrilled about. But she'd nodded yes anyway when Yi Jinsu asked her out to dinner. Because of her name.

"I'll be a soryeong next," he'd joked, looking giddy. He'd just been promoted to captain; next in rank was major, or soryeong, which sounded just like her own name.

Jang Soryeong looked at his buzzed hair and darkly tanned face and gave a little laugh. They'd ordered a sashimi set; the sea urchin that came with it was of

내내 우니를 한 점도 먹지 않았다.

"왜 안 먹어요?"

"안 좋아합니다. 비려요."

기대하던 답이 아니라 조금 김이 샜지만 장소령은 그 날 헤어질 무렵에 "소령님" 하고 장난스레 부르는 이진수의 그을린 얼굴이 그다지 군인처럼 보이지 않는다고 느꼈다. 다음에 만났을 때 장소령은 왜 군인이 되었는지 물었는데, 대답하면서 이진수는 얼굴에 손을 자주 갖다댔다. 생각해본 적 없는 질문이라는 듯이. 장소령은 그냥 알 것 같다고 대꾸했다. 몇 번 만나고 나니 비슷한 점도 있었다. 셔츠를 입을 때 단추를 다 채우는 것이나 누군가 부르는 소리가 들리면 항상 돌아본다는 점이 그랬다. 식사 후 바로 빈 그릇을 치우고 설거지를 한다는 점도 같았다.

이 년 후 그들은 결혼했다. 그로부터 오 년이 지나 이진수는 소령으로 진급했다. 동기에 비해 조금 늦은 편이어서 뭐든 열심히 했다. 얼굴이 그을리고 사택에 들어오는 시간이 점점 늦어졌지만 이진수는 소령에서 멈춰야 했다. 전역 사실을 알리는데 그다지 힘들어 보이지 않았다. 실제로 힘들지 않아서였다. 이진수는 미련

relatively good quality. She put some in her mouth and let it melt on her tongue. Jinsu watched and did not touch another bite of the sea urchin for the rest of the meal.

"Why aren't you eating the sea urchin?"

"I don't care for it. It's too fishy."

It wasn't the answer she was expecting, which left her feeling a little deflated, but later, when they were saying goodbye to each other and Yi Jinsu playfully saluted her as "Soryeong-nim," she decided that his tanned face wasn't as soldierly as she'd first thought. At their next date, Soryeong asked why he'd become a soldier, and Jinsu kept putting his hand to his face while trying to respond. As if the question had never occurred to him before. Soryeong said he didn't have to answer. Several more dates and she noticed similarities. Such as the way they both buttoned their shirts all the way to the top, or automatically turned to look when someone called out. Or the way they both cleared their empty dishes and washed them immediately after eating.

Two years later they married. Five years after that, Jinsu was promoted to soryeong. He was a little behind the rest of his cohort, but he tackled everything with vigor. As the years passed, his face stayed tan, and he returned to company housing later and later each

이 없다고 했다. 오랜 시간 군인으로 지냈지만 두고 온 게 많지 않다는 생각이 든다면서.

"나도 이제 평생 소령이야."

이진수의 농담에 장소령은 웃었다. 이진수가 군인이 아니라고 생각하면 안도감이 들었고 동시에 그의 여전한 짧은 머리와 까만 얼굴, 어중간한 나이를 생각하면, 무엇보다 아들을 떠올리면 조바심이 났다.

처음에 이진수는 이유를 말해주지 않았다. 장소령도 캐묻지 않았다. 저절로 소령에서 중령이 되는 건 아니었다. 시간의 경과를 온순히 누리다가 느닷없이 계급사회에서 탈락하는 사례가 많다는 걸 알았다. 하지만 걸리는 게 있었다. 그간 사택 사람들이 딱한 표정으로 자신을 보던 게 마음에 남았다.

결국 이진수는 얘기했다. 어느 밤, 장소령더러 소파로 와서 앉아보라고 하더니 상사들이 그간 어떤 식으로 물품의 납품단가를 부풀려왔는지, 자신이 어쩌다 가담하게 되었는지, 그 일에 연루된 사람이 부대 안에 얼마나 있는지 얘기했다. 돈이 좀 생겼고 그러자 남다른 활기와 결속력 같은 것도 생겼다. 하지만 거래 내역이 적힌 문서를 본 부하 한 명이 다른 상사에게 고하면서 그

night, but he was forced to stop at soryeong. He did not seem to take the news of his discharge all that hard. And in truth, it wasn't hard. Jinsu said he had no regrets. Though he'd spent so much of his life as a soldier, he said there wasn't much he missed about it.

"Now I, too, am a soryeong for life."

Soryeong had laughed at Jinsu's joke. The thought that he was no longer a soldier brought her some relief, but at the same time, when she considered his still-buzzed hair, tan face, and the fact that he was not getting any younger, she thought about their son and felt impatient.

Jinsu did not tell her at first why he'd been discharged. Nor did Soryeong ask. She knew that one did not automatically get promoted from soryeong to jungryeong. She also knew there were any number of cases of people innocently enjoying the passage of time only to find themselves abruptly eliminated from the hierarchy. But one thing did weigh on her. It was that their neighbors in company housing had been fixing her with looks of pity.

Finally he told her. One night, he invited Soryeong to sit with him on the sofa and told her how his superiors had been inflating the costs of supplies and skimming the extra, and how he had inadvertently found himself joining them, and how many people in his unit were in

일이 알려졌고 책임질 사람이 필요해졌다. 가담자 전원은 아니고 적당한 계급의 한 사람 정도. 그게 이진수였다.

얘기하는 동안 이진수는 내내 벽에 걸린 시계를 보았다. 사 분 걸렸다. 삼 년간 벌어진 일이었는데, 요약하니 간단했다. 장소령은 잠자코 있었다. 화가 나지는 않았다. 이진수가 비교적 솔직히 얘기해줬다는 생각이 들어서였다.

"그게 누구야?"

장소령은 한참 만에 입을 뗐고, 이진수는 중령의 이름을 댔다. 그가 먼저 제안했다. 내키지 않으면 중장비 자격증을 따두는 게 좋을 거라고 했다. 연금 없이 전역하려면 말이다.

"아니, 부하 말이야."

"그걸 알아서 뭐해."

이진수가 퉁명스럽게 군다는 데 장소령은 놀랐다. 틀린 말은 아니었지만 어째서 당당한지 의아했다. 하지만 더 캐묻지 않았다. 어차피 그게 궁금해서 물은 건 아니었다. 달리 할말이 없어서였다. 실망했으나 비난은 쉽고 위로는 가당찮았다. 어린아이에게 하듯 다시는 그러

on it. The money he'd made had filled him with an extraordinary vigor and even a sense of solidarity. But a subordinate who stumbled upon a record of their transactions reported it to one of their superiors; their scheme exposed, someone had to take the fall. Not every someone involved in the scheme, of course, but just one person, of an appropriate rank. That was Yi Jinsu.

While telling her this story, Jinsu had kept his eyes glued to the clock on the wall. It took exactly four minutes. The event itself had taken three years to transpire, but in summary it was all so simple. Soryeong sat there quietly. She did not get angry. Because Jinsu had been relatively honest with her.

"Who was it?" Soryeong asked finally, and Jinsu told her the name of the major who'd suggested that Jinsu take the blame. And if he didn't want to, the major had added, then he better learn how to drive a bulldozer. Because otherwise he'd be losing his pension along with his career.

"No, I mean who was the subordinate."

"What difference does it make?"

Jinsu's tone was sharp, which caught Soryeong off guard. It didn't make any difference, in fact, but she was still surprised at the domineering way he spoke to her. She didn't push. She hadn't asked because she

지 말라고 다짐받을 수도 없었다. 이진수는 홀가분한 표정으로 부엌으로 갔고 장소령 홀로 어리둥절한 기분으로 소파에 남았다.

이후 장소령은 종종 그 밤의 기분을 떠올렸다. 당시에는 이진수가 솔직히 얘기해줬다고 여겼지만 시간이 지날수록 거짓이 포함되었다는 생각이 들었다. 전부는 아니지만 일부는 거짓이라고. 이진수가 자신에 대한 상사들의 처사를 바로 납득해서였다. 그는 책임을 져야 할 사람이 어째서 다른 누가 아니라 자신인지 잘 알고 있는 것 같았다.

이진수는 많은 걸 다시 배워야 했다. 발폭이 EEE로 표시된 군화 대신 치수를 올려 스니커즈를 골랐다. 차체가 낮은 자동차를 제한속도에 유념하며 운전하는 요령을 익혔고 관등성명 없이 전화 받는 습관을 들였다. 딱딱하고 경직된 어미를 쓰지 않고 나이 어린 사람에게도 경어를 쓰려고 했다. 시키기만 하면 다 들어주는 젊은이는 없으며, 지나가는 어린 남자가 자신에게 경례할 리 없다는 것을 의식했다.

그러면서 이진수는 부쩍 늙었다. 그간의 젊음은 줄곧 유지된 짧고 검은 머리와 강마른 얼굴, 단호하고 단일

really wanted to know the answer, she just didn't know what else to ask. It was disappointing, but then again, it was easy to criticize and pointless to try to cheer him up. Nor could she scold him like he was a child and make him promise to never do that again. Jinsu got up and went into the kitchen looking lighthearted, while Soryeong sat alone on the sofa feeling perplexed.

From time to time afterward, Soryeong thought about their conversation that night. She had assumed in the moment that Jinsu spoke honestly, but as the days passed, it occurred to her that part of what he'd told her wasn't true. Not that he had lied to her completely; he'd mixed some lies in with the truth. The way Jinsu had easily accepted his superiors' solution suggested that he knew full well why he had been made the fall guy and no one else.

Jinsu had to relearn everything. He learned to shop for sneakers in a size up instead of army boots marked EEE for extra-wide. He familiarized himself with driving a lower-bodied car while staying mindful of the speed limit and got used to answering the phone without barking out his name and rank. He replaced his brusque, stern way of talking at everyone with softer, polite speech, even when speaking to those younger than him. He came to understand that he could not order younger men around and expect them

한 제복에서 온 모양이었다. 이제 그것들은 없어졌다. 살이 오르면서 이진수는 얼굴이 조금 두툼해졌다. 얼마 전까지 군장을 꾸려 야전훈련을 하던 사람으로는 보이지 않았다. 짧고 직설적인 말투가 여전해서 대출 고객을 상담하는 은행원처럼 보일 때도 있었다. 준비해 간 서류를 일일이 살펴보고 사소한 것을 트집잡아 미진하다며 돌려보낼 듯이 굴었다. 상대를 긴장시키고 실수를 지적하며 깐깐하게 따져 물었다. 긴 인생을 두고 봤을 때 이진수가 군인이었던 것은 잠시뿐이었다. 하지만 인생의 어떤 일은 잠시에 불과할수록 평생 지속된다.

얼마 후 장소령은 상사 부인 중 한 명에게서 걸려온 전화를 받았다. 사택에 있을 때 그녀는 장소령을 제 당번병처럼 부려먹었다. 병사가 있어도 장소령에게 뭔가 시켰다. 장소령이 민망해하는 병사의 눈치를 보는 걸 즐겼다. 한번은 장례식에 가야 하는데 검은색 스타킹이 없다고 했다. "스타킹은 여자가 사야지." 그녀가 말했고, 장소령이 심부름을 다녀왔다.

"자기, 그거 알아?"

"네."

장소령이 대뜸 대꾸하자 여자는 당황했는지 말을 조

18

to obey, and that younger men passing him on the street would not stop to salute him.

Meanwhile, Yi Jinsu aged rapidly. It seemed his youth had come from keeping his dark hair high and tight, his face lean, and his uniform always properly pressed. Now that was all gone. As he gained weight, Jinsu's face filled out. He looked nothing like the man who had up until recently done field training exercises in full gear. He still had a brusque, direct way of speaking, but now he came off more like a bank employee consulting with a customer on loans. Like he might pore over the forms that the customer had so carefully filled out and highlight every minor mistake and hand it back to them, saying their application was incomplete. He would be meticulous in his questioning as he pointed out flaws and make whoever he was talking to nervous. When you considered the whole scope of his life, his time as a soldier had been brief. But sometimes, the shorter a part of one's life is, the more likely it is to last a lifetime.

Not long after that night, Soryeong got a phone call from the wife of one of Jinsu's superior officers. Back when they were living in company housing, this woman had bossed Soryeong around like she was her personal gofer. Even when there was an actual enlisted soldier available, she would give orders to Soryeong

금 더듬으며 "아는구나. 자기가 안다니 다행이네" 하고 말을 이었다.

"아직 입원중이야."

여자가 깊게 한숨을 내쉬었다. 다른 말도 했는데, 이번에는 장소령도 아는 얘기였다. 그렇기는 해도 아는 게 많지는 않았다. 이진수가 왜 그렇게까지 했는지 모르겠다는 여자의 말이 그랬다. "그건 정말 아니잖아." 여자는 또 한숨을 쉬었지만 그 일이 무엇인지 정확히 얘기해주지 않았다.

"자기가 가봐야 하지 않겠어?"

여자가 물었다. 장소령은 누가 입원한 건지, 왜 다친 건지 묻지 않았다. 알면 안 된다는 생각이 들었다. 그 대신 "저는 자기가 아니에요" 하고 더듬거리며 말했다. 여자가 알아듣지 못해 "응?" 하고 되묻더니 화도 내지 않고 그저 습관이라고 얼버무리며 그럼 앞으로 뭐라고 부르냐고 칭얼대듯 물었다.

"소령입니다. 장소령."

장소령은 그대로 전화를 끊어버렸다. 여자는 이름을 말한 줄 모르고 이진수의 계급을 댄 것이려니 여겼으리라.

instead. It had amused her to watch Soryeong squirm and the soldier cringe. One time, the woman had told her she had to attend a funeral and was out of black stockings. "Buying stockings is a woman's job," she'd said, and so Soryeong had gone to fetch them for her.

"Honey, did you know?"

"Yes."

The woman stammered for a moment, probably too caught off guard by Soryeong's quick response, and then said, "So you did know. That's a relief, honey."

With a deep sigh, the woman added, "They're still in the hospital."

She said more, all things that Soryeong already knew. And yet, there was still a lot that Soryeong did not know. She realized just how little she knew when the woman added that she didn't understand why Jinsu had to take it so far. "It's not right," the woman said with another sigh, but she did not specify what "it" referred to.

"Shouldn't you go and see them, honey?" the woman asked.

Soryeong did not ask who was in the hospital or how they got hurt. It occurred to her that maybe it was better that she not know. Instead, she stammered out, "I'm not your honey." The woman responded at first with confusion, but then, without getting angry, gave a

시간이 한참 지나 장소령은 이진수에게 불쑥 그 사람은 어떻게 되었느냐고 물었다.

"누구 말이야?"

이진수가 되물었다. 장소령은 병원에 다녀왔었다고, 다른 사람을 찾는 척 병실에 들어갔었다고 말하지 않았다. 이진수가 그렇게까지 한 결과로 거기서 눈을 감고 누워 있게 된 사람에 대해서도 말하지 않았다.

"글쎄, 무슨 소린지 모르겠네."

이진수는 그렇게 대답하고 슬쩍 일어섰지만 장소령은 그가 알아차렸다는 것을 알 수 있었다.

이진수는 잘해보려고 했다. 돈을 끌어모으고 대로변 건물 일층을 빌려 한우 전문점을 차렸다. 위치 때문에 권리금이 들긴 했어도 저녁식사 시간이면 제법 자리가 찼다. 가게 전면에 숙성고를 배치해서 한우를 덩어리째 넣어뒀다. 군인답게 통이 크다고 말한 사람은 장소령의 아버지였다. 장소령의 아버지는 전역한 이진수를 여전히 소령이라고 불렀다. 장소령에게는 야, 라고 하거나 기집애, 라고 타박하듯 말문을 텄기 때문에 호칭으로 헷갈리는 일은 없었다.

이진수가 군인이었을 때 사택으로 찾아오는 사람들

wishy-washy excuse about how calling people honey was just a little habit of hers and asked in a whiny tone what she should call Soryeong instead.

"Call me Soryeong. Jang Soryeong."

With that, Soryeong hung up the phone. She wondered if the woman would think that Soryeong had given her Jinsu's rank instead of her first name.

After much time had passed, Soryeong asked Jinsu out of the blue what had become of that person.

"Who?" Jinsu asked.

Soryeong did not tell him that she had gone to the hospital and into the person's hospital room by pretending to look for someone else. Jinsu had told her nothing about the person lying in the hospital unconscious as a result of his actions.

"I have no idea what you're talking about," Jinsu said and slunk out of the room, but Soryeong could tell that he'd figured it out.

Jinsu tried to make a go of it. He saved up money and rented the first floor of a building on a busy street and opened a hanwoo barbecue restaurant, serving prime Korean beef. He had to pay a premium for the location, but luckily the tables were full every night. He installed dry-aging refrigerators across the front of the restaurant and filled them with large cuts of beef. Soryeong's father praised the size of the cuts, saying it

이 있었다. 전역 후 자영업을 시작했지만 시간이 지나면 택시나 마을버스 기사 면접을 보러 다니고 이내 얼굴이 검게 변하고 몸이 말라서 돈을 빌리러 오는 사람들이었다. 이진수도 몇 번인가 돈을 줬다. 큰돈은 아니었다. 지갑에 있는 현금을 전부 털거나 근처 편의점 ATM에서 딱 경조사 비용만큼 출금해서 봉투에 넣었다.

"못 받는 돈이야."

이진수의 말이 맞았다. 그 사람들은 더 나빠졌다. 다시 만나본 건 아니었다. 소문으로 들었다. 소문 속에서 그들은 다 잃었다. 돈이 시작이었고 가족 애기로 끝났다. 혹은 가족 문제였는데 파산으로 끝나거나. "어머나, 어쩌다……" 장소령은 애기를 들으면 즉각적으로 대꾸했지만 지나고 나면 마을버스를 몰다 인사 사고를 내서 거액을 물어주고 이혼을 했다는 사람과 결국 빚에 떠밀려 물속으로 차를 몰고 질주했다는 사람이 누구인지 까먹었다. 그 때문에 이진수로부터 영업정지에 대한 애기를 들었을 때도 장소령은 "어머나, 어쩌다……" 하고 대꾸했고 의미를 깨닫고 나서야 흠칫 놀라 입을 다물었다.

befitted a soldier. He still addressed the discharged Jinsu as "soryeong." As for Soryeong herself, she was always "you there" or "girl," as if she could do no right, so there was never any confusion about which one of them he was talking to.

Back when Jinsu was a soldier, there'd been people who came to see him in company housing. After being discharged, he was in business for himself, but it was not long before people came looking to borrow money, people with job interviews to become taxi drivers or bus drivers, their faces drawn and bodies thin. Jinsu gave some of them money. It was never a lot. He would just empty out the cash in his wallet or go to a nearby ATM and take out exactly as much as he would ordinarily give for a wedding or a funeral.

"No one else is going to loan them money," Jinsu said, and he was right.

None of the people he helped got better. He never heard this from them directly, though. Only through rumors, which were always that they'd lost everything. First they lost their money, and then they lost their families. Sometimes it was the other way around. They would start with family problems and end in bankruptcy. With each story, Soryeong automatically exclaimed, "Oh no, what happened…?" But after a while, she could no longer keep track of which person

이진수는 그간 육우를 한우라고 속여 판매해왔다. 단속 때 원산지증명서를 제시하지 못했다. 식당 몇 곳의 이름이 언론에 크게 보도되었는데 그중에 이진수의 식당도 있었다. 영업정지 기간에 식당 정문에 징계 내역과 사과문을 크게 써서 붙여뒀다. 납품업자에게 속은 건 아니었다. 이진수는 알고 했다. 처음엔 찌개와 전골에만 넣었고 나중에는 구이용에도 조금 섞어서 내놓았다.

영업정지 기간이 끝나자 예전처럼은 아니지만 장사가 되기는 했다. 하지만 늘 재료가 남았고 맛이 나빠졌고 당연한 수순으로 손님이 줄었다. 종업원을 해고하면서 장소령이 홀 서빙을 도맡았다. 이진수는 식당에 붙어 있질 않았다. 만회해보려고 다른 일을 벌였고 결국 이번에도 장소령과 소파에 앉아 얘기를 나눠야 했다.

그들에게는 결정해야 할 문제가 있었다. 캐나다에 있는 아들의 거취 말이다. 아이는 일 년 전 어학연수를 떠났고 연수 종료 후 그곳에 있는 학교에 진학했다. "엄마, 여긴 달라요." 아들은 그렇게만 말했다. 장소령은 알아들었다. 장소령은 이진수에게 "거긴 좋대" 하고 바꿔 말했다.

had been driving which neighborhood bus when they hit someone and had to pay a huge settlement and ended up divorced and which person had fallen so far into debt that they drove their car into a lake. And so, when Jinsu told her he had to shut the restaurant down for a while, she automatically murmured, "Oh no, what happened," before realizing what he'd actually said, upon which she went silent with shock.

Jinsu had been swindling their customers, passing off cheaper imported beef as premium Korean beef. During a surprise inspection, he was unable to produce a certificate of origin for the meat. The names of several different restaurants that had been engaged in this sort of scheme were plastered all over the news, Jinsu's included. He posted an apology on the front door of the restaurant, with an explanation of what had happened, and left the sign up for the duration of the closure. This was not a case of a restaurateur being fooled by a supplier. Jinsu knew exactly what he was doing. At first he only served the cheaper beef in soups and stews, but later he started mixing it in with the more expensive cuts for grilling.

When they were able to re-open, business was not like it was before, but they at least got some customers. And yet, every day, there were ingredients left over, and the flavor began to decline, which meant that,

이진수는 아들이 그렇게 말한 건 그곳에 같은 반 아이들이 없어서라고 생각했다. 어떤 밤 아이는 제 방의 이불을 다 찢었다. 어떤 밤엔 제 몸에 볼펜으로 상처를 냈다. 어떤 밤에는 남김없이 토했다. 거기는 적어도 그런 밤이 없다는 뜻이었다.

돌아와야 한다는 말을 어떻게 할 수 있을까. 아침이면 장소령은 아들에게 전화를 걸었다. 안 받을 때가 많았는데, 그런 날은 메시지를 남겨두어도 전화가 다시 걸려오지 않았다. 어쩌다 통화를 하고 끊을 때면 공연히 아들의 이름을 여러 번 불렀다. 아들은 듣지 못한 척 전화를 끊었다. 최근 통화에서는 오랜만에 길게 얘기를 나눴다. 수영을 시작했는데 염소 냄새가 지독하지만 몸이 붕 뜨는 기분이 좋다고 했다. 사람이 많지 않은 시간에 저학년 아이가 풀에 빠져 허우적거리는 걸 도와줬다고도 했다.

"엄마, 걔가 살려달라고 했어. 나한테 그렇게 말하는 사람은 처음 봤어."

아들은 웃었다. 장소령은 본 적 있었다. 두 아이가 무릎을 꿇고 장소령에게 그렇게 말했다. 처음에는 아줌마, 우리한테 왜 그러세요, 라고 했지만 결국 그렇게 말

naturally, they began to lose the few customers they had. They fired their employees, and Soryeong took over waiting tables. Jinsu himself did not hang around the restaurant. He was busy with other work, trying to make up for lost revenue, and it was not long before he and Soryeong had to sit back down on their sofa and have another talk.

There was a problem that needed solving—namely, what to do about their son living in Canada. A year earlier, he had traveled there for language study, after which he enrolled in a local school. "Mom," he'd said, "it's so different here." Soryeong understood what he meant. When she relayed the phone call to Jinsu, she changed the word "different" to "better."

Jinsu assumed their son said so because the kids from his old school were not there. There had been nights when their child tore up his blankets. And other nights when he stabbed himself with a ballpoint pen. And other nights when he could not stop vomiting. His son's words meant that, at least over there, there were no more nights like that.

How, then, to tell their son that he had to come back? Soryeong called him the next morning. He often did not answer his phone; he never called back either, even if she left a voice message. Sometimes, towards the end of a call, she would call out his name several

하게 됐다.

하지만 아들이 떠난 건 그애들 때문이 아니었다. 그런 줄 알고 그애들에게 겁을 줬지만 아니었다. 아들은 알고 있었다. 사택에서 살 때 친구로 지내던 아이에게 전해들었다. 부모들이 방심하고 떠든 얘기를 아마도 아이가 아들에게 옮긴 모양이었다. "엄만 왜 가만히 있었어? 왜 아빠한테 아무 말도 안 했어? 무섭지 않았어?" 느닷없이 아이가 물었던 적이 있었다. 장소령은 아무 대답도 하지 못했다.

"넌 무섭지 않았어?"

장소령이 물었다.

"엄마, 얕은 풀이었어. 가슴까지 왔나? 걜 일으켜세우기만 하면 됐어."

장소령은 그 얘기를 이진수에게 해줬다. 어떤 때는 일으켜세우기만 해도 자기가 넘어진 곳의 깊이를 알 수 있다는 얘기를. 이진수는 잠자코 듣다가 괜찮아져서 다행이야, 하고 말했다. 다 끝나버린 일처럼 얘기했다. 이진수는 아들이 입을 다물고 이불을 찢고 먹은 것을 토하고 방에 틀어박혔던 이유를 끝내 알지 못하리라.

식당을 처분하는 과정에서 애초 이진수가 별 밑천 없

times, in vain. He would pretend not to hear her and hang up. They'd recently had their first long conversation in a while. He told her that he'd started swimming, and though he hated the smell of the chlorine, he enjoyed the feeling of weightlessness. He also told her about rescuing a younger classmate who fell into the pool and couldn't get out. They had been all but alone in the pool together when it happened.

"Mom, he asked me to save him. No one has ever said those words to me before."

He laughed. Soryeong had heard those words before. From the two boys who'd kneeled contritely in front of her. At first they'd said, Lady, why are you doing this to us, but later they'd begged.

Not that they were the reason her son had left. She'd thought so and had scared those children accordingly, but it wasn't the real reason. Her son had found out. He'd heard it from his friends when they were living in company housing. Maybe one of his friends had overheard their parents talking about it during an unguarded moment. "Why didn't you do anything, Mom? Why didn't you say anything to Dad? Weren't you scared?" Her son had surprised her with these questions one day, and she had been unable to respond.

"You weren't scared?" Soryeong asked.

이 대출로 일을 벌였다는 게 드러났다. 담보로 잡혀 있던 아파트도 내놓아야 했다. 다행히 남은 집이 있었는데 매수자가 나타나지 않아서였다. 중개업자에게서 가격 조정 의지가 있는지 확인하는 전화가 걸려오기는 했다. 그다음부터는 똑같았다.

"당신 어떻게 된 거 아니야?"

터무니없는 가격에 이진수가 화를 내고 중개업자와 사이가 틀어져 다른 중개업자를 알아보는 식이었다.

강줄기를 따라 동쪽으로 내려가면 휴양림과 자연 호수가 있는 산이 나타나고, 계곡을 따라 늘어선 조악한 펜션의 반복에 지루할 즈음 건축에 신경쓴 집들이 띄엄띄엄 보이기 시작했다. 그러고도 얼마간 더 들어가야 나무숲에 가려진 그 집이 나타났다.

집을 지은 사람은 제약회사 임원이라고 했다. 퇴직 후 지낼 생각으로 공들였는데 완공 후 얼마 머물지 못했다고. 아내가 아팠다고 했나, 임원에게 문제가 생겼다고 했나. 다른 사람의 일은 아무리 놀라워도 듣고 얼마 지나면 잊어버리고 만다. 아무튼 부부 중 누군가에게 건강 문제가 생겨 오래 머물지 못했고 그후 다시 돌아오지 못했다고 들었다. 어디나 그런 일이 생기니까.

"Mom, the pool's not that deep. It only comes up to maybe my chest? All I had to do was get the kid back on his feet."

Soryeong relayed the story to Jinsu. How, sometimes, simply by standing up, you realized the actual depth to which you'd fallen. Jinsu listened quietly and said, Thank goodness he's doing better. He said it as if that was the end of it. Jinsu would never understand why his son had ground his teeth, torn his blanket, vomited everything he ate, and locked himself in his room.

In the process of closing the restaurant, it was revealed that Jinsu had been floating the business on loans with almost no seed capital of his own. The apartment, which he'd used as collateral, had to be put on the market as well. Luckily for them, they still had the vacation house, as no buyers had appeared yet. They did keep getting phone calls from the real estate agent, though, asking if they were willing to drop the price. Each phone call went the same way.

"Are you out of your mind?"

Jinsu would lash out at the agent over the absurdly low price, and as the relationship soured, he'd start looking for other agents.

If you headed east along the river, you would reach a mountain with a lake and a recreational forest, and just as you were growing bored of the endless row of

누군가 문제가 생겨 집을 떠나고, 일단 떠나면 다시 돌아오기 힘들어지는 일 말이다.

그다음 주인은 식자재 납품업자였는데, 그가 채무를 제때 해결하지 못하면서 이태 전 이진수가 헐값이나 다름없는 조건으로 넘겨받았다. 이렇게 뺏길 집이 아니라고 납품업자가 눈물을 흘렸다. 조금만 봐달라고, 기다려주면 갚을 수 있다고도 했다. 이진수는 개업 때부터 그와만 거래를 했다. 채소들을 다 그에게 받아 썼다. 그는 시간에 늦는 법이 결코 없었고, 주문하지 않은 물건을 매번 덤으로 주고 갔다. 품질이 나쁜 경우가 거의 없었는데, 장마가 길어지거나 가뭄으로 물건이 나빠지면 어떤 식으로든 보충해줬다. 진상품마냥 믿음직스러운 사람이었다. 얼마나 믿음직스러운지 이진수가 돈도 빌려줬던 것이다. 상환이 곤란해졌지만 시간을 주면 충분히 해결할 수 있다고 한 말도 믿었다. 하지만 이진수는 원칙대로 했고, 장소령의 아버지에게 수완이 좋다는 말을 들었다.

한 번쯤 이런 곳에 살아봐도 좋겠다는 생각이 드는 집이었다. 하지만 입때껏 두 사람이 이곳에 살지 않은 것은 그럴 마음이 없었기 때문이었다. 간혹 아는 사람

shoddy pensions lining the valley, a scattering of houses would appear, houses that had put a lot more care into their design. A bit further on, obscured by trees, was their vacation home.

They'd been told the house was built by a pharmaceutical company executive. He had put a great deal of work into the house, thinking that he and his wife would live there after retirement, but they did not stay long once it was completed. Either his wife got sick or something happened to him. It's always the case that no matter how shocking other people's problems are, we forget the details soon after hearing about it. At any rate, health problems struck one of them, forcing them to move back to the city, after which they were unable to return. It could happen to anyone. Something goes wrong and you have to leave your home, and once you're out, it becomes that much harder to go back.

The next owner was a food supplier. When he couldn't pay down his debts on time, the house went to Jinsu for practically nothing. That was two years ago. The supplier had wept, saying how unfair it was that his house was being stolen from him like this. Have mercy, he'd pleaded, he just needed a little more time and he would be able to pay it all back. When Jinsu opened the restaurant, he dealt exclusively with the

에게 집을 빌려주고 고맙다는 말을 듣기도 했다. 연휴 때면 빌려달라는 사람이 많아 오히려 양해를 구해야 했다. 이제 그런 연락을 해오는 사람은 없었다.

아이가 있을 때는 자주 이곳에서 주말을 보냈다. 제법 먼길을 걸어 인근 사찰에 다녀오거나 계곡에서 낚시하는 사람들을 구경했다. 물이 깊고 유속이 빨라 입질이 좋다고 들었는데 그래서인지 낚시하는 사람이 많았다. 이진수와 아이도 몇 번인가 함께 낚시를 했다. 이진수는 금세 지루해했지만 아이는 끈기 있게 낚싯대를 들고 기다렸다. 작은 민물고기가 걸려 환호성을 지르자 근처 낚시꾼들이 조용히 하라면서도 아이를 칭찬해주었다. 고기의 이름이 갈겨니라고 가르쳐주기도 했다. 양동이에 갈겨니를 담아 오다 말고 아이는 장소령에게 도로 가서 풀어주자고 했다. 그런 날이면 괜찮다는 생각이 들었다.

이진수는 집 왼편 마당에 차를 댔다. 배드민턴을 칠 수 있을 정도로 넓은 마당이었다. 차에서 내린 이진수가 어수선한 마당을 둘러보고는 주저앉아 흙을 만져보았다.

"여기에 뭔가 심을까? 상추 같은 걸로. 그건 싸고 빨

supplier. All of his vegetables came from him. The supplier was never late and always threw in freebies that weren't on the order form. His products were almost never poor quality, and when the rainy season dragged on too long or a drought damaged the produce, he never failed to find a way to make up for it. In terms of trustworthiness, he was the genuine article. So trustworthy, in fact, that Jinsu even loaned him money *and* believed he meant it when he swore he'd find a way to repay Jinsu, somehow, if Jinsu would only give him a little more time. But Jinsu also stuck to the rules, and Soryeong's father praised him for his business acumen.

It was the kind of house that most people wished to live in full-time at some point in their lives. Not that the two of them ever had. They lacked the desire. They loaned the place out to friends every now and then, accepting only thanks in exchange. They got so many requests from friends wanting to borrow the house on holiday weekends that they had to turn people away. Not that they got any of those calls anymore.

Before their son left, they'd spent many a weekend there. They would take long walks to visit a Buddhist temple nearby or watch people fishing in the stream. People said the water in the stream was deep and fast, which made for good fishing, and that must have been

리 자라잖아."

"원래 노지 상추가 맛있어."

한가하게 상추나 심을 때인가 싶었지만 장소령이 맞
장구쳤다. 기분과 상관없이 뭔가 키우는 일은 늘 도움
이 되니까.

시간을 들여 청소부터 하고 다저녁이 되어서야 호박
과 감자, 청양고추를 넣어 얼큰한 칼국수를 끓여먹었
다. 그러고는 낡은 리클라이너에 앉아 어두워진 계곡을
내려다보고 있자니 조금 기운이 나면서 쉬러 온 기분마
저 들었다.

다음날 장소령과 이진수는 종묘상에 들러 모종을 사
왔다. 종묘상 주인에게서 아무리 텃밭이라도 비닐 멀칭
을 해야 한다는 말을 여러 번 반복해서 들었지만 무시
했다. 돌을 고르고 물을 적셔가며 흙을 다듬은 후 포트
에서 모종을 빼내 간격을 두고 심었다. 목이 마르면 갓
끓인 보리차를 입으로 불어가며 식혀 마셨다. 주말에는
날이 좋아서 계곡으로 내려가 낚싯대를 드리운 사람들
을 구경하다 돌아왔다. 어떤 날은 햇빛 비치는 창가에
할 일 없이 앉아 졸다가 양푼에 나물을 넣고 잔뜩 밥을
비벼 이진수와 나눠 먹기도 했다. 화훼농원에 가서 포

why so many people went there to fish. Jinsu and his son had also fished there a few times. Jinsu always bored of it quickly, but their son would wait patiently, holding the fishing pole. Once, he pulled up a small fish and cheered with excitement only to be scolded by the other fishermen for being too noisy, even as they praised him for his catch. They told him the fish was called a dark chub. On the way home with the little fish in his bucket, their son suddenly suggested to Soryeong that they go back and release it. On days like that, she thought maybe their child was going to be okay.

Jinsu parked the car in the yard to the left of the house. It was a big yard, spacious enough for playing badminton. He stepped out of the car, took one look at the messy yard, and squatted down to feel the dirt.

"What should we plant here? Maybe lettuce. It's cheap and grows fast."

Soryeong wondered whether they really had the leisure to sit around growing lettuce, but she chimed in anyway and said, "Lettuce grown on open ground does taste good." After all, regardless of how you were feeling, it was always helpful to grow something.

They took their time cleaning. It was well into the evening before they finally got around to making dinner: a spicy noodle soup with squash, potato, and

치 근처에 둘 화분도 여럿 사왔다. 지저분한 화분 겉면을 물로 깨끗이 닦아 나무 크기에 맞춰 늘어놓았다. 꽃이 피는 것들은 화분에서 꺼내 마당 한쪽에 심었다. 그러는 동안 집은 살림집 모양새를 갖춰갔고, 얹혀사는 기분이 드는 와중에도 이런 가을이 부디 끝나지 않았으면 싶은 마음도 생겼다.

며칠 지나자 부동산 중개업자가 찾아왔다. 중개업자는 곧장 휴대전화를 꺼내 집안 여기저기를 사진으로 찍었다. 점심을 먹느라 꺼내놓은 그릇들을 빤히 보아서 이진수가 재빨리 그릇들을 수납장에 집어넣었다.

"이만하면 관리가 잘된 셈이네요. 경기가 안 좋아도 살 사람은 사거든요."

중개업자가 말했다. 중개업자의 판단이 시세를 결정하기라도 하는 것처럼 이진수의 기분이 좋아 보였다. 그래서인지 본심과 다른 말도 했다.

"기왕이면 좋은 분한테 팔아주세요."

"좋은 분이 따로 있나요. 제값 주고 사면 좋은 분이죠."

중개업자가 말했고 이진수가 자신의 생각도 그렇다는 듯 고개를 끄덕였다.

chili peppers. Then they sat in their old recliners and looked out at the darkening valley, feeling at last that they were there to relax and recharge.

The next day, Soryeong and Jinsu dropped by the seed store to purchase some seedlings. The seed shop owner warned them several times that, even for a simple kitchen garden, they still needed to cover the rows with plastic mulch, but they ignored him. They cleared stones, watered the soil, and smoothed it out as they went, then removed the seedlings from their pots and planted them at even distances from each other. When they grew thirsty, they sipped freshly brewed barley tea, blowing on it to cool it. The weather was good that weekend, so they took a walk to watch people casting their fishing lines into the stream. On some days, with nothing else to do, Soryeong would bask in the sunlight pouring through a window and doze off, then wake to mix a big heaping of rice with seasoned greens in a large brass bowl, which she would eat with Jinsu. She went to a flower farm and bought several items to plant near the porch. She hosed off the dirty pots and wiped them clean, then lined them up by size. She removed the flowering trees from the pots and planted those in the yard. Meanwhile, the house began to look more like a home, and though she couldn't quite shake the feeling that

매매가를 낮추자 예상보다 빈번하게 사람들이 들렀다. 중개업자와 함께이거나 중개업자 없이 성별과 차림이 각기 다른 두세 명이 불쑥 찾아왔지만 사려는 사람보다 그저 봐두려는 사람들로 보였다. 집을 보러 오는 사람들은 흠을 잘 찾아냈다. 정남향은 해가 너무 비쳐 못쓴다는 말도 들었다. 사진 액자를 가까이 들여다보며 아들은 어디 갔냐고 묻는 사람도 있었다. 계곡물 소리가 들리자 창호를 트집잡았고 여간하면 눈에 띄지 않는 비뚤어진 줄눈을 가리키며 시공 실수라고 지적했다.

거래 중지는 아니고 며칠만 방문객 없이 지내보자고 장소령이 말했다. 이진수도 고개를 끄덕였다. 하지만 중개업자에게서 전화가 걸려오자 이진수는 상의 없이 약속을 잡았다. 중개업자는 서울서 오는 사람들이라 좀 늦을 거라면서, 그래도 가도 되느냐고 물었고 이진수는 언제라도 편할 때 방문하라고 대답했다.

오후가 되자 비가 쏟아지기 시작했다. 꿉꿉한 냄새가 풍겨서 비가 들이치는데도 한참 현관문을 열어두었다. 이진수는 열린 문 앞에 구부정하게 앉아 상추를 심은 밭이 빗줄기에 속절없이 파이는 것을 지켜봤다. 종묘상 주인의 말대로 아무래도 헛수고를 한 것 같았다. 빗물

they were living in someone else's home, she also found herself wishing that this autumn would never end.

A few days later, the real estate agent came to visit. He took out his cell phone and began taking photos of the inside of the house. As the agent eyeballed the lunch dishes sitting on the table, Jinsu hurried to hide them in a cabinet.

"The house looks like it's been fairly well taken care of," the agent said. "The economy's not great, but someone will want to buy it."

Jinsu looked happy, as if the agent's judgment alone would boost its market value. Perhaps that was why he said the opposite of what he was really feeling.

"In that case, please sell it to a good person."

"Is there such a thing? Whoever pays the asking price is a good person, am I right?"

Jinsu nodded, as if he agreed.

With the asking price lowered, more people began to stop by. Small groups of two or three, of varying genders and dressed very differently from each other, sometimes accompanied by an agent and sometimes not, would drop in unexpectedly, but they seemed more like looky-loos than potential homebuyers. They enjoyed pointing out the house's flaws. With the house facing dead south, they said, the sunlight was far too

이 포치 안쪽까지 튀었다.

바깥에서 차 소리가 들렸다. 이진수가 재빨리 일어나 현관 밖으로 나갔다. 각자 커다란 우산을 든 남자 둘이 막 차에서 내렸다. 이진수는 남자들이 몰고 온 차가 상추밭을 깔아뭉갠 것을 보았지만 아무 말도 하지 않았다.

한 남자가 우산을 펼치지 않고 대뜸 포치로 뛰어들어왔다. 다른 남자는 느긋이 걸어왔고 포치에서도 펼쳐진 우산을 접지 않았다. 두 사람은 조심성 없이 양복 상의를 털고 집안으로 들어섰다.

방을 보여줄 때마다 남자들은 잠자코 고개만 끄덕였다. 사실 별 관심이 없어 보였다. 이런 날 굳이 내려왔으면서 정작 집 내부를 둘러보는 일에는 건성이었다. 남향인지 동향인지, 계곡과 가까운데 너무 습하지 않은지 묻지 않았다. 세면대 수도를 틀어보지 않았고 보일러실이 어디에 있는지 다용도실에 곰팡이가 슬지 않았는지 체크하지 않았다.

"이건 꼭 보셔야 해요."

이진수가 욕실에 설치된 편백나무 욕조를 가리켰다. 거기에서는 특별한 향이 풍겼다. 장소령은 좋아하지 않

intense. One person stared closely at their framed photos and asked where their son was. Then, when the person noticed that the sounds of the stream carried all the way into the house, he complained about the windows and doors, pointing out crooked joints that would normally have gone unnoticed, and blamed it on poor construction.

Soryeong suggested to Jinsu that they stop showing the house for a few days—not to stop the sale but to take a little break from visitors. Jinsu nodded. But when he got another call from their agent, he went ahead and agreed to the appointment without consulting her. The agent asked whether it would be okay for the prospective buyers to arrive a little late since they were coming from Seoul, and Jinsu said they were welcome to stop by any time they liked.

That afternoon, it began to rain. The smell of dampness filled the house, so they left the front door open to air it out, despite the rain that came in. Jinsu sat hunched over in front of the open door and watched his lettuce garden being helplessly pounded by rivulets of rain. Just as the seed shop owner had warned him, their hard work had been for nothing. The rain ricocheted all the way up to the porch.

He heard a car pull up. Jinsu hurriedly rose and stepped outside. Two men, each holding large

는 냄새였다. 두 남자가 살짝 인상을 썼다. 이진수는 못 보았는지 욕조에 대해 장황하게 말했다. 한 남자가 이 진수를 빤히 보며 열심히 들었다. 다른 사람은 욕실 이 곳저곳으로 눈을 돌렸다.

보여줄 건 다 보여줬다. 이진수는 그들이 집을 둘러 보며 조금 흥미를 보인 것들, 거실 층고나 외벽 자재, 건축가의 이름 같은 것을 되풀이해 말했다. 호감을 사 는 데 필요한 정보라고 여기는 것 같았다.

"생각해보고 중개사 통해 연락하겠습니다."

내내 딴청을 부리던 남자가 말했다. 장소령은 그 말 이 무슨 의미인지 알아차렸다. 누군가와 상의하지 않고 스스로 결정할 수 있지만 당장 계약할 만큼 마음에 들 지 않는다는 뜻이었다.

"혹시 소령님 아니십니까?"

이진수를 쳐다보던 남자가 좀더 다가오며 물었다. 이 진수는 뒤로 물러서지 않으려 애쓰며 눈을 가늘게 떴 다.

"접니다, 박민옵니다. 박일병이요."

이진수가 어색하게 그를 보았고 어, 어, 하고 당황한 듯 기억을 더듬다가 자네군, 하고 톤을 높여 말했다. 누

umbrellas, were getting out of the car. Jinsu saw that their car had trampled right over his lettuce plants, but he said nothing.

One of the men rushed onto the porch without opening his umbrella. The other took his time, and left his umbrella open even after he was on the porch. They both carelessly swept the rain off of their suit jackets and entered the house.

The men nodded halfheartedly as Jinsu gave them a tour of each room. They did not look the least bit interested. Their indifference was surprising, considering they'd come all this way and in this weather. They did not ask whether the house faced south or east, or if the proximity to the stream made the house too damp. They did not turn on the taps or check the location of the boiler or whether the utility room had mold.

"You'll definitely want to see this."

Jinsu showed them the hinoki-wood tub in the bathroom. The fragrance of the cypress filled the small space. Soryeong did not care for the scent. The two men frowned slightly, but Jinsu was too busy droning on about the bathtub's merits to notice. One of the men stared at Jinsu, listening carefully as he spoke. The other kept looking around at the rest of the bathroom.

Jinsu had shown them everything there was to see.

군지 떠올랐다기보다는 우선 그렇게 말해둘 필요가 있다고 여긴 듯했다. 그런 일이 종종 있었다. 이진수는 기억하지도 못하는 사람들이 다가와서 이진수의 계급을 대며 인사를 하고 자기 소개를 하는 일. 식당으로 고기를 먹으러 와서 아는 체한 사람도 있고 동네 슈퍼마켓이나 찜질방에서 인사를 받기도 했다.

박민오는 허리를 숙여 인사하고 장소령에게도 인사를 건넸다. 선 채로 조금 나눈 대화를 통해 이진수는 그들이 법인 명의로 주택을 구매한다는 사실을 알게 되었다. 나쁘지 않은 소식이었다. 어차피 이런 집은 생활 감각으로 따져 묻지 않아야 살 수 있었다. 편의시설이 멀다거나 인적이 드문 걸 단점으로 치지 않고, 골프장과 가까워 좋다는 사람들에게 어울리는 집이었다.

"오랜만인데 차라도 한잔하고 가지."

이진수가 손을 내밀었다. 박민오가 손을 맞잡으며 옆에 있는 남자를 쳐다봤다. 남자는 바깥을 내다보고는 그러는 게 좋겠다고 했다. 비가 어지간히 퍼붓고 있었다.

"아무래도 차 말고 술이 낫지? 오랜만인데 아쉽잖아."

He kept reiterating certain details: whatever they'd shown a glimmer of interest in, as well as other things like the height of the living room ceiling, the material used for the exterior walls, the name of the architect. He seemed to think this information was necessary for creating a good impression.

One of the men, who'd been especially resistant to Jinsu's sales pitch, kept saying, "We'll give it some thought and contact you through our agent."

Soryeong knew what that meant. They could make up their minds on their own without having to consult anyone, but they weren't enamored enough with the house to sign a contract then and there.

The man who'd been staring at Jinsu stepped closer to him and said, "By the way, weren't you the soryeong-nim?"

Jinsu narrowed his eyes and made an effort to not retreat from the man.

"It's me, Bak Mino. Private Bak."

Jinsu's expression turned awkward, and he muttered to himself, "Uh, uh," as if searching his memory, before finally saying, in a high-pitched voice, "It's you." It was obvious that he had no idea who the man was but felt he ought to say something. It was hardly the first time this had happened to him. He'd been approached before by people he didn't remember only to have

장소령이 찻물을 불에 올려놓자 이진수가 말했다. 이진수는 대답할 시간을 주지 않겠다는 듯 냉장고에서 와인부터 꺼냈다. 저녁에 먹으려고 내놓은 소고기도 꺼냈다. 차를 가져왔다고 말하면서도 두 남자는 더 말리지 않았다.

이진수는 달군 팬에 두태 기름을 고루 바르고 등심 조각을 올려놓았다. 시간을 두고 핏물이 사라진 고기를 한 번 뒤집어 익히고 남자들 쪽으로 밀어주었다. 서울에서 고깃집을 한다고 하자 박민오는 대뜸 "그럼 이 한우가 소령님이 파시는 거예요?" 하고 물었다. 이진수는 느긋한 표정으로 웃었다. 한입 가득 고기를 넣고 우물거리며 박민오가 과장되게 엄지손가락을 들어올렸다. 남자는 아랑곳없이 묵묵히 먹었다.

여전히 이진수는 박민오가 누군지 기억나지 않는 듯했지만 집을 팔고 사는 일을 화제로 삼는 건 즐거워 보였다. 박민오와 남자는 여러 채의 건물과 집을 거래해왔다. 그게 그들의 일이었다. 거액의 건물을 사서 법인의 세금을 줄이고 차액을 남겨 되파는 일 말이다. 그 일에 관심이 있음을 보이고 싶어서 이진수는 매매 기준이 뭐냐고 물었다.

them greet him by his former rank and introduce themselves. He'd been recognized by customers at the restaurant and greeted by strangers in their local supermarket and sauna.

Bak Mino bowed to Jinsu and greeted Soryeong, too. As they stood around talking, Jinsu learned that the two men were looking to purchase a house in the name of their company. That wasn't unwelcome news. After all, it was the type of house that you could only buy if you weren't too concerned about the inconvenience of its location. It was a good house for people who would not consider the lack of nearby stores or restaurants a drawback, people who would appreciate its proximity to a golf course.

"It's been so long since we last saw each other. How about some tea or coffee before you go?" Jinsu asked, holding out his hand for a belated shake.

Bak Mino took his hand and gave a look to the man standing next to him. The man glanced outside and agreed. The rain was still coming down hard.

"On second thought, how about some wine instead?" Jinsu asked, just as Soryeong had set a kettle of cold water on the stove. "It'd be a shame not to have a drink together after all this time."

He pulled a bottle of wine out of the refrigerator without giving Soryeong time to respond. He also

"간단해요."

남자가 말했다.

"예산이죠."

이진수는 남자가 제 이름도 말해주지 않은 것을 깨달았지만 허허 웃었다. 박민오가 왜 아까운 집을 팔려느냐고 물어 이진수는 서울에서 좀더 가까운 곳으로 알아보고 있다고 둘러댔다. 나이들수록 가까운 게 좋다고, 멀리 있으면 멀어지는 법이라고도 했다.

운전을 해야 한다면서 술을 마시지 않던 두 남자는 금세 의지가 약해졌다. 처음에는 입에 잔만 댔고 향이 좋다며 한 모금 마셨고 이럴 바에는 빨리 먹고 깨는 게 낫다고 했고 단속이 없는 곳이라면서 조금 더 마셨고 와인이 떨어지자 아무거나 좋다고 해서 소주를 내놓자 그것을 마셨다.

"그나저나 자네들 그건 알고 있나?"

"뭐요?"

"내가 심어둔 상추랑 채소를 자네들이 차로 죄다 깔아뭉갰어."

"죄송합니다, 소령님. 미처 못 봤습니다."

박민오가 벌떡 일어나 장난스레 거수경례를 했다. 장

pulled out the beef that she'd been planning to cook for dinner. The men made some vague protests about having to drive back, but they did not stop him.

Jinsu heated up a tabletop grill, brushed on an even layer of cooking oil, and started cooking slices of sirloin. When the meat browned, he flipped each piece over to finish cooking and pushed it over towards the men. He told them he'd owned a barbecue place in Seoul, and Mino said, "Oh, so this is the beef you served?" Jinsu smiled in response. Mino took a bite of the grilled steak and gave an exaggerated thumbs up. The other man ate silently, indifferent to the conversation.

It was clear that Jinsu still did not remember who Mino was, but he seemed to enjoy talking about buying and selling houses. Mino and the other man had purchased several homes and buildings. That was their job. Buying a building for a large amount of money, reducing the company's taxes, and then reselling it for a tidy profit. Wanting to show an interest in their work, Jinsu asked what their criteria was for making a purchase.

"That's simple," the other man said. "Whatever fits our budget."

It occurred to Jinsu then that the other man had not told him his name, but he laughed anyway. Mino asked

소령은 박민오가 고기 여러 점을 한꺼번에 입에 넣고 질근질근 씹는 것을, 입에 든 것을 보이며 말하고 웃는 것을 지켜보았다. 이진수가 여전히 소령이었다면 박민오와 테이블에 마주앉아 고기를 구워먹는 일 따위는 없었을 것이다.

"아주 힘들게 심은 거야. 풀이 좀 있어야 집이 더 잘 보일 테니까. 여기 나무가 아주 근사해. 현관 앞 소나무는 울진에서 가지고 왔지."

현관은 닫혀 있고 마당은 보이지 않는데도 세 사람은 일제히 그쪽으로 고개를 돌렸다. 어둡지만 무엇인가 보인다는 듯 얼마간 그쪽을 쳐다봤다.

"자네들도 안목이 있으니 비만 안 왔어도 대번에 알아봤을 거야. 날 좋을 때 꼭 다시 오라고."

"집은 이런 날 보는 겁니다."

남자가 대꾸했다.

"응?"

이진수가 웬 농담이냐는 듯 되물었다.

"나무도 풀도 꽃도 없을 때 봐야 집이 제대로 보여요."

"아니지. 이런 집은 산세랑 물길, 햇빛과 나무가 어떻

why Jinsu was selling such a lovely home, and Jinsu said he wanted to move a little closer to Seoul. That as he grew older, he found it better to be close to the city, and that the distance seemed to only worsen with time.

The two men who'd said they shouldn't drink since they had to drive soon loosened their inhibitions. At first they merely touched their lips to the rim of the glass and said the wine had a nice bouquet, but that quickly turned into a tiny sip, followed by the declaration that since they'd come all this way they may as well drink it down fast, to give themselves more time to sober up, and since the police didn't patrol for drunk drivers all the way out here, why not have a little more, and soon enough the wine was gone but anything was fine with them, including, yes, soju, which they drank.

"By the way, do you fellas know what you did?"

"What did we do?"

"You crushed my lettuce garden with that car of yours."

"Our apologies, soryeong-nim," Bak Mino said, springing out of his seat and giving Jinsu a playful salute. "We had no idea."

Soryeong watched as Mino stuffed several pieces of meat in his mouth at one time, chewing it with his mouth open, talking and laughing as he ate. Had Jinsu

게 자리잡았는지가 중요하지. 다 보고 제대로 사야지."

남자가 피식 웃으며 되물었다.

"집을 잘 아시네요? 겨울엔 안 살아보셨죠?"

이진수는 당황해서 남자와 박민오를 번갈아 보았다. 박민오는 재미있다는 듯 남자를 쳐다봤다. 박민오는 웃기까지 했다. 소리 내어 웃은 건 아니고 슬쩍 미소 지었다. 나이 어린 남자가 이진수의 기분을 거스르는 일은 별로 없었다. 이진수는 줄곧 대접받으며 지내왔다. 기분이 상하면 다시 그러지 않도록 가르쳐주면 그만이었다. 그럴 수 없어서 이진수는 잠자코 고기를 먹기 시작했다. 쉬지 않고 먹었다. 핏기가 가시기 무섭게 집어먹었다.

"소령님은 정말 제가 기억나세요?"

박민오가 얼굴이 붉어져서 물었다.

"그럼, 그럼. 다 기억나지."

이진수가 건성으로 대꾸했다. 집 얘기를 꺼내기 곤란해진 후로 이진수는 눈에 띄게 지루해하고 있었다.

"다행이네요. 하긴 잊으면 안 되죠. 소령님 덕에 우린 좀 좋아졌잖아요."

박민오가 말했다.

still been a soryeong, there was no chance Mino would have been invited to sit at this table with them, grilling meat together like this.

"It was a lot of work planting that lettuce. A house needs some greenery around it to look good. The trees here are magnificent. Those pine trees next to the front door were brought all the way from Uljin."

The three men turned to look in unison even though the front door was closed and the windows revealed nothing. They stared in the same direction as if they could see something out there despite the darkness.

"You fellas have a good eye, so you would have spotted them yourselves if it weren't for the rain. You ought to come back when the weather's good."

"This is the best weather for looking at houses," the other man said.

"Is it now?"

"It's easier to see a house for what it is without any trees, flowers, or grass."

"No, no. A house like this, you have to see how the mountains, the water, the sunlight, and the trees are all situated, too. You have to take it all in before you decide."

The man smirked and said, "So you think you know this house? Have you tried living here in the winter?"

Flustered and annoyed, Jinsu looked back and forth

"허허, 그랬나?"

"소령님이 다른 부대로 가시고 육사 출신 대위가 대대장으로 왔거든요."

이진수가 박민오를 쳐다봤다. 그러고 보니 보급대에 있던 병사인 모양이었다. 시기를 특정해도 기억이 나지 않기는 마찬가지였지만.

"소령님이 멀리서 걸어오시기만 해도 우린 다 쫄았어요."

이진수가 기분좋게 웃었다. 그는 권위와 위계를 칭찬으로 여겼다.

"우릴 엄청 팼으니까요. 툭하면 팼어요. 우리더러 악마에 씌었다고 했어요."

박민오는 키득거렸지만 이진수의 표정은 굳었다. 이진수는 덕분에 좋아졌다는 말을 그제야 알아들었다. 남자는 "그때야 다 그랬지" 하고 짐짓 대수롭지 않게 대꾸했다. 이진수가 남자의 말에 조금 여유를 되찾고 "다 그랬지" 하고 따라 말했다.

"다 그렇긴요. 대대장님은 안 그러셨어요. 일병 시절은 정말 끔찍했어요."

박민오가 주머니에서 휴대전화를 꺼냈다.

at the two men. Mino looked at his companion as if he were enjoying himself and smiled. Actually, it was more of a smirk than a smile. It was rare for Jinsu to encounter a younger man bold enough to offend him. Jinsu was used to being treated a certain way. In the past, whenever he'd found himself offended, all he had to do was enlighten the other person as to what they'd done wrong. But since he could not do that now, he went back to eating without saying another word. He continued eating without pause. He plucked the pieces of meat from the grill nearly before they had finished cooking.

"Soryeong-nim, do you really remember me?" Mino asked, his face reddening.

"Yeah, sure, of course, I remember you," Jinsu said absentmindedly. Now that it was harder to keep the conversation focused on the house, Jinsu's energy was visibly flagging.

"That's good. But, of course, how could you forget me? You made our lives better."

"Ha, did I now?"

"Because you left for another unit, and the captain from the military academy became our battalion leader instead."

Jinsu stared at Mino. He must have been stationed with the supply battalion. Not that Jinsu would have

"아직도 제가 누군지 모르시죠? 그러면 사진을 찍어둘까요? 사진을 보면 다 떠오르잖아요."

"이런 꼴을 찍어서 뭐한다고……"

이진수가 제 차림을 살폈다. 박민오는 아랑곳 않고 사진을 찍고는 들여다봤다. 이진수에게 보여주지는 않았다.

"사진에는 별의별 사람들이 다 남아 있잖아요. 나를 때린 사람도 있고 내가 잘못한 사람도 있고요. 심지어 죽은 사람도 있어서 기분이 이상해져요. 소령님도 그렇죠?"

박민오가 사진을 보며 무표정하게 물었다. 왜 없겠는가. 이진수의 아버지는 삼 년 전에 죽었다. 장소령의 친정어머니는 그보다 일찍 죽었다. 누구에게나 그런 사람이 있다. 하지만 이진수는 대꾸하지 못했다. 대신 딱딱해진 고기 한 점을 입에 넣고 천천히 씹었다.

별안간 장소령은 박민오가 남편을 처음 소령님이라 불렀을 때 느낀 거북스러움이 무엇 때문인지 깨달았다. 박민오는 허리를 구부려 인사했다. 사회에서 만난 연장자에게 하듯이. 군인의 방식은 아니었다. 오랜만에 만난 사람들은 뭔가에 빨려들듯 그 시절의 말투와 행동으

remembered him even if he'd specified the year.

"All you had to do was walk toward us from a distance and we'd be shaking in our boots."

Jinsu smiled happily. For him, wielding authority and outranking others were synonymous with receiving praise.

"We were scared of you because you beat the hell out of us all the time. You'd beat us at the drop of a hat. You said we were possessed by the devil."

Mino chuckled, but Jinsu's face hardened. Jinsu understood now what Mino had meant when he said that he'd made their lives better. The other man shrugged it off, saying, "That's how things were back then." Jinsu relaxed a little at his comment and echoed him, saying, "That's how things were."

"No, they weren't. The new battalion leader never beat us. We really suffered under you." Mino pulled his cell phone from his pocket and aimed the camera at Jinsu. "You still don't remember who I am, do you? Shall I take a photo? I think it'll all come back to you once you see a photo."

"Why would you take a photo of me dressed like this…?"

Jinsu looked down at his clothes. Unfazed, Mino took a photo anyway and studied it. He did not show it to Jinsu.

로 돌아가지 않나. 소령과 일병이던 시절로 말이다.

"난 있어요."

남자가 말했다.

"고향에서 제일 친한 친구였어요. 항상 셋이 붙어다
녔죠. 하루는 내가 어딜 가느라 빠지고 두 녀석만 산에
갔죠. 그런데 한 친구가 굴렀어요. 굴렀는데 목에 시퍼
렇게 멍이 든 거예요. 맨날 가는 산인데 하필이면 다른
길로 가서 거기서 굴렀죠. 그런데 이상하죠. 사람이 굴
렀다면서 구조 신고도 바로 안 했더라고요. 어떻게 그
럴 수 있죠? 병원에 오래 있었는데 결국 못 깨어났어
요."

이진수는 눈살을 찌푸렸다. 그는 자주 그런 표정을
지었다. 뭔가를 정확히 보려거나 깊은 생각에 빠져서
그렇게 하는 건 아니었다.

"그래서 내가 산을 싫어해요. 나무도 싫어하고 계곡
도 싫고요."

남자가 갑자기 웃었다. 박민오도 따라 웃었다. 뭐가
웃긴 걸까. 장소령은 두 사람이 그저 술을 많이 마셨다
고 생각하기로 했다.

고기가 팬 위에서 타들어갔다. 냄새가 났다. 이젠 아

"There are all kinds of people who live on in photographs. People who beat me, and people I wronged. There are even dead people, which feels strange. Don't you agree, soryeong-nim?"

Mino's face as he studied the photo was unchanging.

Why wouldn't they have photos of the dead? Jinsu' father died three years ago. Soryeong's mother died before that. Everyone had someone who'd died. But Jinsu did not respond. He just stuffed another piece of overcooked meat into his mouth and chewed it slowly.

It occurred to Soryeong suddenly—the reason she had felt uneasy when Mino first addressed her husband as soryeong-nim. He had bowed from the waist. No different from how any civilian would greet an elder. But not how a soldier would do it. And didn't people usually revert to old habits and mannerisms when meeting someone they once knew, as if being sucked back into something? Especially when that something was the days of being a private versus a major.

"I've got a photo of a dead man," the other man said. "He was my best friend from back home. There were three of us who did everything together. One day, I couldn't join for some reason, so the two of them went hiking alone. Somehow he slipped. He fell off a ledge, and ended up with his neck all black and blue. We used to go up that mountain all the time, but for some

무도 고기에 손을 대지 않았다. 화력을 조절하지도 않았다. 장소령은 육즙이 다 빠져 딱딱해진 시커먼 고기를 쳐다보았다.

"죽은 친구랑 같이 산에 갔던 친구가요, 자기는 매주 예배를 보러 간대요. 예배가 끝나면 꼭 봉사도 한대요. 식당에서 교인들한테 밥도 퍼주고 청소도 한대요. 예배당 바닥도 닦고 길쭉길쭉한 의자도 죄다 걸레로 닦고 교회 마당에서 쓰레기도 줍고 비질도 하고 계단도 쓴대요. 비가 올 때는 비를 맞으면서 그걸 다 한대요."

그는 이진수를 빤히 쳐다봤다.

"자긴 그걸로 다 됐대요. 충분하대요."

말을 마친 남자가 애당초 입을 연 적 없다는 듯 무표정한 얼굴로 돌아갔다. 박민오가 그런 남자를 보더니 키득거렸다. 얼굴을 구기며 웃어서 우는 것처럼 보이기도 했다.

"소령님도 그럴 때가 있어요?"

박민오가 눈가를 닦으며 물었다.

"있어요? 뭘 했어요?"

"하긴 뭘 해. 자네들 그만 일어나지. 너무 취했어. 대

reason, on that day, they took a different path, and he fell. But you know what the really weird part is? The other guy said he fell, but he didn't call for help right away. How could that be? My friend was in the hospital for a long time but never woke up."

Jinsu frowned. It was a face he made often. And not because he was trying to get a better look at something or because he was deep in thought.

"That's why I hate the mountains," the other man said, with an unexpected laugh. "I hate trees, too, and mountain streams."

Mino laughed, too. What was so funny? Soryeong figured the two men must have simply had too much to drink.

The meat was burning. It smelled. No one was eating it now. No one turned the heat down on the grill, either. Soryeong stared at the blackened pieces of meat, turned tough from where the juices had all run out.

"That guy who went on that hike with my dead friend, he says he goes to mass every week now. After mass ends, he does volunteer work. He works in the church kitchen, serving food to the other parishioners, and helps clean. He scrubs the floor of the chapel, wipes down all those long pews, picks up trash in the

리를 불러야겠어."

"나는 부하가 아니잖아요."

남자가 소리쳤다. 이진수가 놀란 표정을 지었다. 틀린 말은 아니었지만 장소령도 놀랐다.

"에이, 가긴 어딜 가요. 술도 남고 고기도 이렇게 남았는데요."

박민오가 어리광을 부리듯 말했다.

"다 먹었어. 자네 많이 했네."

"다 먹고 이거 다 치우고 가겠습니다. 상추도 다시 심고 가겠습니다. 어디 지금 치워 볼까요?"

박민오가 빈 그릇을 들고 자리에서 비틀거리며 일어섰다.

"아니야, 괜찮아. 그냥 둬. 아무것도 하지 마."

"왜요? 왜 아무것도 안 해요? 뭐라도 해야죠."

박민오가 이진수를 빤히 보았다. 그는 이제 웃지 않았다. 울지도 않았다.

"그래, 알았으니까 그만들 가지."

"왜 계속 반말이냐고. 나는 부하가 아니라고."

남자가 이진수에게 다시 말했다. 박민오가 낄낄 웃으

churchyard and sweeps it clean, and he even sweeps the stairs. When it rains, he says he does it all in the rain, too."

He stared hard at Jinsu, and added, "He says that's all he needs to do. That it's enough."

The man's face went slack, as if he hadn't just spoken. Mino looked at him and chuckled. The way his face wrinkled as he laughed made it look like he was crying.

"Do you have something like that, too, soryeong-nim?" Mino asked as he wiped his eyes. "Do you? What do you do?"

"What *would* I do? I think it's time for you fellows to leave. You've had too much to drink. Let's call you a driver."

"You can't order me around," the man said, raising his voice. "I am not one of your men!"

Jinsu looked shocked. The man wasn't wrong, but Soryeong was also surprised by his outburst.

"Aw, come on, why would we leave now?" Mino whined playfully. "There's plenty of alcohol left, and all this meat, too."

"The meat's done. You two have had plenty."

"We'll leave after we've finished eating and cleaning up. We'll replant your lettuce, too, on our way out.

며 그를 일으켰다. 이진수는 한숨을 쉬고 현관으로 걸어가 재촉하듯 문을 열었다. 장소령이 어떻게 가려느냐고 묻자 박민오는 무작정 문가를 가리켰다. 어둡고 폭우가 내리는 마당에 그들의 차가 있었다. 그들은 취했고, 이 상태로 다른 곳으로 가지 못할 것이다. 대리기사가 오기를 기다리거나 어쩌면 밤새 거기 있을지도 몰랐다.

이 집은 넓고 방이 여러 개였지만 장소령은 그들에게 방을 내줄 생각이 없었다. 사람들은 제가 지내는 곳으로 돌아가야 했다.

"그런데 소령님."

박민오가 현관을 나서다 말고 불렀다. 남자는 휘청거리는 걸음으로 인사도 없이 요란한 빗속으로 걸어나갔다. 포치의 조명 때문에 그의 젖은 어깨가 번들거렸다.

"소령님."

박민오가 다시 불렀다. 장소령과 이진수가 동시에 그를 쳐다보았다. 박민오가 뭐라고 말했다. 포치에 떨어지는 빗소리가 워낙 요란해서 취한 듯 중얼거리는 박민오의 목소리는 들리지 않았다. 남자는 폭우가 내리는

Where shall I put the plates?"

Mino got up with a plate in his hand, stumbling as he went.

"No, it's fine. Just leave it. Don't do anything."

"Why? Why don't you want us to do anything? We have to do something."

Mino stared at Jinsu. He was not smiling anymore. Nor was he crying.

"Okay, okay, I got your message loud and clear. It's time for you to go."

"Why are you still ordering me around?" the other man repeated. "I told you I'm not under your command."

Mino chuckled and helped the other man up. Jinsu let out a sigh, walked over to the front door, and held it open, to usher them out. Soryeong asked how they were planning to get home, and Mino pointed out the door. Their car was still there, of course, parked in the darkened yard, in the pouring rain. But the men were drunk and in no shape for driving. They would have to call for a driver to come, or else stay the night.

The house was spacious and there were plenty of bedrooms, but Soryeong had no desire to offer them one. People ought to return to wherever they lived.

"By the way, soryeong-nim," Mino said, pausing on

어둠 속에 우두커니 서서 장소령과 이진수가 있는 쪽을 빤히 쳐다보았다.

"예? 소령님?"

박민오가 목소리를 높였다. 이진수가 느긋하게 뒷짐을 졌다. 장소령은 박민오가 애타게 부르는 소령님이 누구인지, 무엇을 추궁하려는지 당연히 알았다. 하지만 아는 체 하지 않았다. 좀더 시간이 지나봐야 정확히 알 것 같았기 때문이다.

his way out the front door. The other man had already stumbled outside, into the rain, which was coming down as loudly as ever, without so much as a goodbye. The porch light made his wet shoulders glisten.

"Soryeong-nim," Mino called out again.

Soryeong and Jinsu turned to look at him in unison. Mino muttered something. But his drunken slurring was not audible over the drumming of the rain on the porch. The other man stood in the dark, getting pelted by the rain, as he stared hard at the couple.

"Well, soryeong-nim?" Mino asked, raising his voice.

Jinsu looked relaxed as he clasped his hands behind his back. Soryeong knew full well which soryoeng-nim Mino was so anxiously calling out to, as well as what he was asking. But she pretended not to know. Because it was only a matter of time before she knew for certain.

해설
Commentary

내몰린 사람들

인아영(문학평론가)

편혜영의 소설에는 내몰린 사람들이 있다. 무엇으로부터? 자신이 소속되어있는 특정한 단체나 조직으로부터, 혹은 기묘하게 얽혀있는 주변 사람들로부터, 혹은 그저 이 세계로부터. 이들은 자신이 폭력적인 세계에 내던져졌고 약육강식이라는 촘촘한 그물에 걸려있으며 아무리 애를 써도 이 거대한 부조리에서 벗어날 수 없다는 사실을 동물적인 감각으로 알고 있다. 견고한 위계서열로 구축된 이 세계는 공정하지 않다. 유리한 사람과 불리한 사람, 무감한 권력자와 억울한 피해자는 한 무대 위에 엉겨 있다. 점점 나빠져가는 사태의 진상은 선명하게 떠오르지 않고 다만 그 사태에서 내몰린

People Pushed Out

In A-yeong (Literary Critic)

   Pyun Hye-young's work abounds with people who
have been pushed out. Of what, you ask? Out of the
communities or organizations to which they belong,
out of the strangely intertwined relationships that
surround them, or simply out of the world itself. They
are thrown into a world of violence, trapped in a finely
woven web in which the weak are prey and the strong
are predators, and made aware, in the way that animals
are aware, that no matter how hard they try they can
never escape this colossal absurdity. This world,
constructed atop an unshakeable hierarchy, is not fair.
The privileged and the unprivileged, unfeeling
wielders of power and wronged victims alike, share the
same stage. And the truth, that this situation only grows

사람의 표정이 밀착되어 드러난다. 거기에서 편혜영의 소설은 시작된다.

「홀리데이 홈」에서 그 내몰린 사람은 이진수다. 군인이었던 이진수는 아내 장소령을 처음 만날 때쯤 대위에서 소령으로 진급하지만, 결혼 후에 군대 내 납품단가 조작 사건에 가담한 책임을 홀로 떠안고 전역한다. 전역 후에는 권위주의적이고 수직적인 군대의 규범으로부터 벗어나 부드럽고 수평적인 사회의 관행을 몸에 익히려고 하지만 그리 쉬운 일이 아니다. 이진수는 한우 전문점을 차려 생계를 유지해보려 하지만 육우를 한우라고 속여 판매하는 바람에 영업정지를 당하고 결국에는 식당을 처분하게 된다. 그뿐만 아니라 식당을 개점할 때 받았던 대출이 불안정했음이 드러나면서 담보로 잡혀있던 아파트도 잃고 만다. 악화를 거듭하는 상황에서 마지막으로 남은 교외의 집을 처분하려던 중 집을 보러 온 남자들이 이진수의 군대 후임이었음이 밝혀지면서, 언뜻 건조하게 보였던 원한과 폭력의 기미가 고요한 표면 아래에 맹렬하게 들끓기 시작한다.

흥미롭게도 소설은 이진수에게 구체적으로 무슨 일이 있었는지 거의 드러내지 않는다. 군대 내 납품단가

worse, is not revealed clearly; instead, we see up close only the expressions of those driven to this state. This is the starting point of Pyun Hye-young's stories.

In "Holiday Home," the person pushed out is Yi Jinsu. A former soldier, Jinsu is promoted from captain (*daewi*) to major (*soryeong*) around the time he meets his future wife, Jang Soryeong, but at some point after they are married and raising a son, he is implicated in an embezzlement scandal and made to take the fall alone. After being discharged, he is freed of the authoritarianism and vertical hierarchy of military life, but he struggles to learn the customs of a soft, horizontally-oriented civil society. Jinsu tries to make a living by opening a barbecue restaurant that advertises premium Korean beef, but is caught swindling customers by passing off cheaper beef instead. His business is first temporarily suspended and then forced to close entirely. On top of that, he is unable to repay the loan he used to open the restaurant and must sell their apartment, which was held as collateral. In the midst of this downward spiral, he tries to sell their second home outside the city. There, he is visited by two men, prospective house buyers, who turn out to be Jinsu's former subordinates in the military. Sly hints of resentment and violence lurking beneath the calm surface of their interaction begin to heat up and boil

조작 사건에 연루된 사람들이 많았는데도 왜 그것을 책임지고 전역한 사람은 이진수 한 명이었는지, 이진수는 왜 그 사실에 부당함을 느끼지 않고 아내 장소령에게 그것을 당당한 태도로 말했는지, 거래 내역이 적힌 문서를 보고 고발한 부하는 누구였는지, 왜 누군가가 이진수 때문에 병실에 눈을 감고 누워 있게 되었는지, 이진수가 "그렇게까지 한" 일은 정확히 무엇이었는지, 그리고 이진수의 교외 집을 보러 온 박민오와 남자는 군대에 있던 시절 이진수에게 어떤 일을 당했는지, 소설은 일일이 설명하지 않는다. 다만 이진수와 장소령이 공들여 심은 상추밭을 깔아뭉개는 자동차, 입안에서 여러 점의 고기를 질근질근 씹으면서 웃는 박민오의 모습 등의 이미지를 통해 이진수의 과거에 저질렀던 폭력이 박민오나 남자와 연관되어 있을 것이라고 서늘하게 짐작케 할 뿐이다.

그러나 어쩌면 그런 것들은 중요하지 않다. 오히려 중요한 것은 이진수에게 구체적으로 무슨 일이 일어났는지와 무관하게 소설이 견고한 형식으로 짜여있다는 사실, 다시 말해 이진수가 저지른 행위의 구체적인 내용이 텅 비어있다는 사실 자체다. 왜냐하면 이 부조리

over.

Interestingly, the story makes almost zero mention of what actually happened to Yi Jinsu. Given how many people were involved in the embezzlement scandal, which entailed manipulating the prices of military supplies, why was Jinsu the only one made to take the blame and get discharged for it? Why did Jinsu accept this without feeling wronged and tell his wife about it with such confidence? Who was the subordinate who discovered the records of their fraudulent transactions and reported it? Why was someone hospitalized and in a coma because of Jinsu, what exactly was it that Jinsu "took too far," and what happened between Jinsu and the two visitors back when they were in the army? The story answers none of these questions. We can only guess from the images in the story—of the car crushing the lettuce plants that Jinsu and Soryeong had so carefully planted, of Bak Mino laughing while chewing a mouthful of meat, and of other moments—that the violence in Jinsu's past may be connected to Mino and his companion.

And yet, maybe none of that matters. Instead what does matter is the form of the story itself, the fact that it is woven solid, with no regard for what happened to Jinsu—or to put it another way, the fact itself that the specifics of what he did are empty. This is because the

한 세계가 휘두르는 무력이란 인간으로 하여금 내용이 아닌 형식에 복무하게 만들기 때문이다. 그렇기 때문에 이 소설의 밑바탕은 시키는 대로 따라야 하는 상명하달의 원칙이 지배하고 수직적인 권위체계가 집약되어 있는 군대라는 공간인 것이다. 그런 배경에서 훈련받고 자신을 형성해온 이진수는 부조리를 부지불식간에 학습하고 그 관행을 그대로 체화한다. 그래서 이진수에게는 딜레마가 없다. 자책도 억울함도 없다. 단지 "권위와 위계"를 칭찬으로 여길 뿐이다. 적어도 소설의 표면에서, 이진수는 시스템과 분리되지 않는다.

그런데 이러한 사건들은 왜 이진수의 아내인 장소령의 시선으로 담기고 있는 것일까. 내몰리는 사람의 내면이 아니라 바로 그 옆에 있는 사람의 시선으로 말이다. 이진수에 대한 장소령의 반응과 거리감에는 묘한 구석이 있다. 장소령은 이진수가 행해온 폭력에 직접적으로 연루되진 않았지만 그렇다고 그와 완전히 무관하지도 않다. 결혼 전 첫 만남에서부터 군인다운 이진수의 모습에 미약한 불안함을 느끼지만, 이후에 이진수가 자신에게 무언가를 솔직하게 고백하지 않을 때마다 반응을 뭉갠다. 불길함은 감지하면서도 사태를 적극적으

force wielded by an unjust world makes people serve form, not content. Hence, the backdrop to this story is the military, with its intensely vertical system of authority and principle of top-down leadership, which demands that one does as one is told. Having been trained and formed in this crucible, Jinsu unwittingly absorbs its absurdity and carries out its customs. Thus, for Jinsu, there is no dilemma. No guilt or injustice, either. Quite simply, he regards "authority" and "rank" as nothing more than compliments. On the story's surface, at least, Jinsu is inseparable from the system.

The question that remains is why the story is told from the point of view of Jinsu's wife, Jang Soryeong. That is, not from the point of view of the person who is being pushed out but from that of the person at his side. There is an aspect of mystery to Soryeong's reactions to her husband and the distance between the two of them. Soryeong was not an accomplice to Jinsu's wrongdoings, and yet she is not entirely innocent either. Though she felt a faint stirring of unease at Jinsu's soldierly appearance on their first date, whenever Jinsu later withholds part of the truth from her, she suppresses any response. Even while sensing that something is not right, she asks no questions. Perhaps, then, the central dilemma of this story is not Jinsu's, with his absorption into military culture, but rather

로 따져 묻지 않는다. 그러니 어쩌면 이 소설에서 던져진 딜레마는 애초에 군대의 조직 문화를 흡수한 이진수의 것이 아니라 그런 이진수와 자신이 얼마나 다른지 확신하지 못하는 장소령의 것이다. 마지막 장면에서 박민오가 애타게 이진수를 추궁하는 모습을 보면서도, 이 모든 사태를 정확히는 모르겠다는 장소령의 목소리는 그녀가 놓인 자리를 말해준다.

그렇기에 학교폭력으로 인해 캐나다 어학연수를 간 것으로 보이는 아들이 장소령에게 묻는 질문, 그리고 집을 보러온 남자가 절친한 친구들의 이야기로부터 출발해 이진수로 가닿는 추궁은 의미심장하게 공명한다. "엄만 왜 가만히 있었어? 왜 아빠한테 아무 말도 안 했어? 무섭지 않았어?"라고 장소령에게 묻는 아들과 "소령님도 그럴 때가 있어요?" "왜요? 왜 아무것도 안 해요? 뭐라도 해야죠."라고 이진수에게 묻는 남자. 왜 가만히 있었냐고, 왜 아무것도 안 하냐고 묻는 이들의 질문은 제대로 알 수도 없는 잘못을 추궁한다는 점에서 섬뜩한 것이 아니다. 섬뜩한 것은 이진수의 언행을 한 발짝 떨어진 곳에서 보며 미온한 불안감을 느껴온 장소령이 이진수에게 던져진 바로 그 질문에 함께 처하고

Soryeong's, as she cannot fully differentiate herself from her husband. Even while watching Mino grill her husband with questions in the final scene, Soryeong's insistence that she does not know the whole story speaks to her position.

Therefore, Soryeong's phone call to their son who is studying abroad in Canada, presumably to escape being bullied back at home, and their visitor's story about his best friend's death resonate meaningfully. Their son asks her, "Why didn't you do anything, Mom? Why didn't you say anything to Dad? Weren't you scared?" Their visitor asks, "Do you have something like that, too, soryeong-nim?" and "Why? Why don't you want us to do anything? We have to do something." What unsettles the reader is not this interrogation of unspoken wrongdoings. Rather, what's unsettling is knowing that Soryeong, who feels a lukewarm anxiety while observing everything her husband says and does from a mere step away, is just as much a target of these questions. In a world without exits, we all end up wearing the same face. And that is the true horror of Pyun Hye-young's stories.

있다는 것이다. 출구 없는 세계에서 우리는 결국 똑같은 얼굴을 하고 있다. 편혜영의 소설에서 정말 무서운 것은 그런 것이다.

비평의 목소리
Critical Acclaim

K

편혜영은 2000년에 등단하여 다섯 권의 소설집과 다섯 권의 장편소설을 낸 바 있다. 짧지 않은 시간 동안 꾸준히 다채로운 이야기를 만들어내었지만 기괴하고 불편한 이미지로 가득 찬 재난과 파국의 서사는 여전히 편혜영 소설의 대표적 인상으로 남아 있다. 그리고 그 재난과 파국의 선연하고 섬뜩한 이미지들은 꽤 오랫동안 세기말을 말하는 2000년대 한국 소설의 중요한 어법으로 여겨져왔다.

이미지로 극대화된 세계의 불안과 공포는 그 대상과 서술의 방법을 달리한 이후에도 여전히 잔상처럼 남아 소설의 인상을 결정하고 있는 것이다. 물론 그것은 잔

Since her literary debut in 2000, Pyun Hye-young has published five short story collections and five novels. This has included diverse and wide-ranging works, but she is still primarily known for stories of catastrophe and collapse, replete with uncanny and discomforting images. In fact, those vivid and terrifying images of catastrophe and collapse have long been regarded as keywords for explaining fin-de-siecle Korean literature.

In a world magnified by images, fear and anxiety linger like an afterimage, even after the subject and narrative mode have changed, determining the impression of her work. Of course, it is not really an afterimage at all, but the result of a tenacious, cool-headed pursuit and exploration of the dark side of the

상이 아니라 이미지로 대리되지 않는 세계의 이면에 대한, 집요하고 냉담한 탐색과 추적의 결과물이다.

서영인, 「몰락에 대하여─편혜영의 최근 소설들」, 『문학과사회』 제32권 제4호, 문학과지성사, 2019. 209~224쪽.

살아가는 일을 두렵게 바꾸는 이 낯선 지옥도가 실상 병원처럼 우리의 곁에 있으면서, 매일 우리의 일상을 만드는 원리임을 편혜영을 따라 걷다보면 천천히 깨닫게 될 것이다.

편혜영 소설의 긴장감은 위태로운 사건이 만들지 않는다. 소설의 긴장은 사건에 의해서 연장되지만, 가장 끔찍한 두려움은 불투명하게 남겨진 사건의 진실에서 오지 않고, 잔인한 현재에 자신이 복무하고 있다는 뒤늦은 깨달음에서 온다.

편혜영이 직시한 공포는 지금도 웃는 얼굴로 누군가의 어깨를 토닥이며 편안하게 그 자리에 앉도록 만드는 능숙한 일상의 기술이고, 그 적당한 압력에 의해 가닿은 심연의 어둠이다.

김요섭, 「나는 그 자리에 남았다─편혜영 소설 속 '병원─제도'의 불안」, 『문학동네』 제26권 제2호, 문학동네, 24쪽.

world that does not lend itself to being substituted with images.

Seo Young-in, "On Ruin: The Recent Works of Pyun Hye-young," *Literature and Society, Vol. 32, No. 4.,* **Moonji Publishing, 2019, pp. 209-224.**

When you begin to walk with Pyun Hye-young, you realize that this unfamiliar road to hell that puts us in fear of life is, in fact, always nearby, the way a hospital is always close, and is identical to the principles that form our daily lives.

The tension in Pyun Hye-young's work is not created by scenes of danger. Instead, that sense of danger prolongs the tension, but the true horror comes not from those unresolved events but rather from the belated realization that one is bound in service to a merciless present.

The horror that Pyun Hye-young confronts is the handy everyday skill of tapping on someone's shoulder with a smile and inviting them to take a seat, and the darkness of the abyss that is felt in that most delicate of pressures.

Kim Yo-seop, "I Stayed Behind: The Anxiety of 'Hospitals and Institutions' in Pyun Hye-young's Work," *Munhakdongne, Vol. 26, No. 2,* **Munhakdongne, p. 24.**

K-픽션 028
홀리데이 홈

2020년 12월 28일 초판 1쇄 발행

지은이 편혜영 | 옮긴이 김소라 | 펴낸이 김재범
기획위원 전성태, 정은경, 이경재, 강영숙
편집 정경미 | 관리 홍희표, 박수연 | 디자인 다랑어스토리
인쇄·제책 굿에그커뮤니케이션 | 종이 한솔PNS
펴낸곳 (주)아시아 | 출판등록 2006년 1월 27일 제406-2006-000004호
주소 경기도 파주시 회동길 445(서울 사무소: 서울특별시 동작구 서달로 161-1 3층)
전화 02.821.5055 | 팩스 02.821.5057 | 홈페이지 www.bookasia.org
ISBN 979-11-5662-173-7(set) | 979-11-5662-521-6
값은 뒤표지에 있습니다.

K-Fiction 028
Holiday Home

Written by Pyun Hye-young | Translated by Sora Kim-Russell
Published by Asia Publishers | 161-1, Seodal-ro, Dongjak-gu, Seoul, Korea
Homepage Address www.bookasia.org | Tel.(822).821.5055 | Fax.(822).821.5057
First published in Korea by ASIA Publishers 2020
ISBN 979-11-5662-173-7(set) | 979-11-5662-521-6

K-픽션 한국 젊은 소설

최근에 발표된 단편소설 중 가장 우수하고 흥미로운 작품을 엄선하여 출간하는 〈K-픽션〉은 한국문학의 생생한 현장을 국내외 독자들과 실시간으로 공유하고자 기획되었습니다. 원작의 재미와 품격을 최대한 살린 〈K-픽션〉 시리즈는 매 계절마다 새로운 작품을 선보입니다.